The Quest

The Untold Story of Steve, Book One - The Tale of a Hero

By Mark Mulle

PUBLISHED BY:

Mark Mulle

Copyright © 2014

TABLE OF CONTENTS

Book One: The Tale of a Hero

My name is Steve, and I am the hero of this world. There's something about the single-player mode that makes me feel this way. I am in charge of my own destiny, and no one else can change that. You may think it's a lonely experience, but that's not the case. My wolf companion, Growls, is the only friend I need. I spend my days building a grander house and keeping the monsters at bay. There's some joy to be had fighting zombies alongside Growls and brushing skeletons off my lawn. I've earned my right to thrive in this world, and none can stop me.

Lately though, something weird has been going on. I've been coming across different structures that look like a player made them. There were fenced-in areas, half-built wooden houses, and railways outside of the caves leading to nowhere. To my knowledge, none of these were randomly generated by the game. It was probably a new update I didn't know about. Which was fine by me. Just more things to explore, I decided.

Today I decided to go out and explore beyond the forest near my home. I wandered my way into what looked like the makings of a wooden house. It appeared to be abandoned just as the roof was being built. It had a few one-block windows, and the floor was a mix of dirt and grass. Inside was a bed, a few torches, and a single treasure chest. Maybe there were some goodies left behind like some iron, a saddle, or maybe even some armor. Curiosity dictated I open it. The chest cracked open with a familiar creak. All I found inside was a single book someone had already written in. I picked it up and began to read.

It will not be long now until I reach the end.
It guides me there. I don't know why.
I can feel it watching every move I make.
To be honest, I am scared.
I feel if I make the wrong move, it'll end me.
I don't know what to think anymore.
I thought I was playing a g—

My reading was cut short as a creeper snuck up on me. I respawned in my bed, frustrated at the loss of my items. I scrambled to get back to the house and reclaim everything. I rummaged through the forest, thankful that I left a trail of torches along the way. The house faded into view within a few minutes. Although it was more of a hole than a house. I was able to find all of my old items, however the book I was reading was gone. Strange—I didn't think books could be destroyed by a creeper explosion. It must've been a new update. That's a shame, I thought; there were a few more sentences left. What I did read was odd though. Kind of cryptic. Plus there was no author. It must have been an Easter egg or something left by the developers. I shrugged it off and made my way back home.

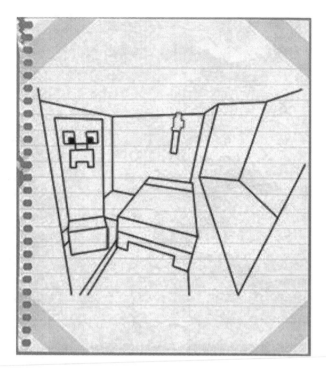

    I followed the torches back to my homestead. My house wasn't very big yet, but it was humble and polished with a colonial theme. I was in the process of building a fence around it to help keep the monsters out, but it was not finished yet. I had Growls wait for me on the front porch. I tossed him one of my cooked pork chops, and we both headed inside for the night. As I stored some of my items away, I could hear the zombies approach. Their incessant moaning had always irked me. They started banging on my door. Watching the door crack just a little bit put me on edge every time. I played on normal difficulty so I knew they wouldn't be able to break in, but that didn't make it any more unnerving. Still, I always ended up blockading the door with a few dirt blocks just to be safe. I lay down on my bed and passed away the night.

Or so I would have liked. The game woke me in the middle of the sleep sequence with the message saying: *You may not rest now, there are monsters nearby*. I looked around my house in a panic, but there was nothing there. I ran to the nearest window to see if the zombies were still there. But the clearing where my house was nestled in was bare. Not even any skeletons or creepers in sight. No hostile mobs in the middle of the night? What was this—a glitch? I went back to the bed to try to sleep again. When I clicked on it, the same message appeared: *You may not rest now, there are monsters nearby*. I clicked the bed a few more times in irritation. After the twelfth click it let me rest, and I woke up again in the daytime.

I dug out the dirt blockade and ventured cautiously outside. There weren't any rotten flesh or bones that usually littered my yard when the sun rose. Weird—I thought there would be at least something dropped from the zombies banging on the door, but the yard was void of items. I glanced up to make sure there were no spiders on the roof. It was all clear. Growls followed me as I checked the perimeter of the house. No sneaky creepers nearby either. It was as if the mobs never spawned at all. I was a little concerned, but I had to put the thought behind me. Daylight was being wasted.

I realized I was getting low on wood. I ran back inside my house and grabbed my axe from the chest. I then headed to the forest between my house and the abandoned one. I mindlessly hacked away at each block of wood, working from the ground up. The leaf blocks were destroyed in hopes they would yield saplings to plant. Whatever I took from this world, I tried to give back. If I chopped down one tree, I'd plant two more at the very least. I could just destroy each tree and leave a barren wasteland in my wake, but that wasn't me. The forest was a landmark as well as a valuable resource, and even though it was just a game, I respected it.

I carried sixty-four blocks of wood back to my house and proceeded to craft more fencing. After forty-three pieces were made, I took what I had and resumed my work on my fence. To my satisfaction, the fence was completed with a few pieces to spare. I ran back inside to craft more torches. Each one was then placed on each post of my fence. Monsters didn't spawn when there was a lot of light, and I did not want to take any chances of them spawning inside my fence. As the last torch was placed, I could see the sun setting. Growls and I retreated inside and helped ourselves to some steak. All in all, a productive day.

I waited for the sun to set. Watching from my window, it was clear to see that the fence had done its job. I could see the mobs beginning to spawn. The spiders, I knew, would be able to climb over. I could handle them. The zombies, skeletons and creepers, however, were all kept out. Now that was a success. I was ready to turn in for the night, quite pleased with myself. It wasn't until I reached my bed that I remembered whom I had forgotten.

The enderman. The teleporting terror of my nightmares. It easily bypassed my fence and now wandered around the outside of my house. *Don't look at it*, I chanted to myself. *Just let it do what it wants. If it wants to take a piece of my house or some dirt, okay. I can fix that. Just don't look at it.* There are so many things about the enderman that frighten me. Its eyes, its voice, the way it emanates that weird purple smoke. Or what happens when you look it in the eye. I shivered at the thought. This was the only mob that made me feel unsafe inside my own house. My next goal was to definitely find a way to repel the endermen from my home.

I was able to sleep through the whole night without any worry of monsters nearby to my great relief. Some searching online had shown me that endermen didn't particularly care for water. I decided to dig out some dirt rows inside my fence and fill them with water. It would help keep the endermen away, and I'll be able to build that garden I had wanted to make for a while. I was hitting two birds with one stone. Lines of wheat, carrots, and potatoes danced in my head as I dug. The rows were finished by sunset.

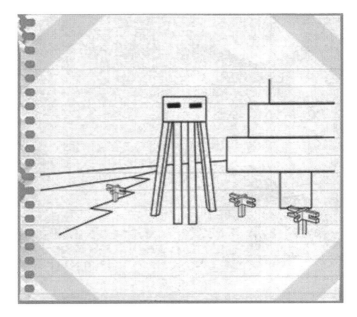

Over the next few days, I spent my time gathering water with my buckets and filling the rows around my house. I crafted a hoe from some iron ingots I had stored away and proceeded to till the land. I filled half of the rows with plain seeds I gathered in the forest. The other half was filled with carrots and potatoes that I, um, "borrowed" from a nearby village. In my defense, I did not take all of their food. I'm not that kind of guy. Anyway the sun had gone down already, but I was so close to finishing that I decided to just keep going despite the danger. I looked over my handiwork when it occurred to me that the mobs hadn't spawned again. No zombies, skeletons, creepers, or spiders. I found this a little disturbing, so I decided it would be best to head inside. When I turned around there was a lone enderman who had made its way inside my fence. What was peculiar though was that it was standing in one of my rows of water. It wasn't taking damage or teleporting away as it should have been. Without even thinking, I made a huge mistake. I looked at its face.

Its jaw unhinged, and it stared me down. I could hear that god-awful static noise reverberate with every fiber of my being. My heart began to race, and I was too afraid to move. As the noise got louder and louder I could feel my anxiety reach its peak. I couldn't look at it any longer. It teleported behind me and knocked off a good chunk of my health. I switched to my sword and swung at it, clipping it slightly as it teleported again. The enderman came at me in a rage until I was down to three hearts of health. It seemed like this particular enderman was stronger than the others I had faced previously. My sword was the only tool made of diamond in my arsenal, and this should have been a fair fight. It was like my game had switched itself from normal to hard difficulty. This wasn't going to end well, so I resigned to my fate. Suddenly, Growls came rushing toward the enderman, eyes blood red. He viciously attacked the enderman until it teleported away. My eyes darted all around to see where it went, but it was nowhere to be seen. A small breath was finally able to escape me. Growls and I made our way inside my house where I fed us some cooked chicken. Growls earned himself a second helping.

It had been a few days since the rogue enderman incident. I decided to redo the roof of my house with glass. They seemed to have taken on the role of main nuisance now that the endermen had more trouble getting through my garden. I headed to the east of my house where there was a small beach. With my sturdy iron shovel in tow, I began to gather blocks of sand. When I had a full stack, it was time to head back home. Walking back to the clearing, I caught something out of the corner of my eye. At first it seemed like a shade of green, and I immediately thought: creeper. I whipped my head around to get a better look at it. I had a chance to see that it wasn't really a green but more of a teal, but by the time I turned my head it was gone. It probably was just a creeper. In any case I hurried back to my house.

As my house was coming into view, I noticed something strange. There was a chest by the gate of my fence. There was no memory of leaving a chest there. I ran up to it and threw it open. Inside was a single written book. Another one? I thought. I took it out of the chest and began to read. After a few sentences it was clear that this was the same book as the one in the abandoned house. It still had no author. I puzzled over how it could have made its way into a chest by my fence. This seemed to be a little more than an Easter egg. My confusion was instantly overshadowed by my anxiousness to see what else the book had to say.

It will not be long now until I reach the end.
It guides me there. I don't know why.
I can feel it watching every move I make.
To be honest, I am scared.
I feel if I make the wrong move, it'll end me.
I don't know what to think anymore.
I thought I was playing a game.
But the game is breaking.
It rewrites the rules.
It wants to see what I do.
It wants to see what you do.
Don't drown in the brine.

I closed the book and placed it back inside the chest. My thoughts were swirling around those words. What could they have possibly meant? It seemed like it was written by another player, but how could it have made its way to my single-player world? Was someone tampering with my game? That would explain a lot of the glitches I had encountered. This must have been some really elaborate prank by some hacker. Well, the first thing I should do, I thought, is bring up these glitches on the forums. I needed to see if anyone else had experienced these things.

I had typed out all that had happened to me so far. The mysterious structures, the mobs not spawning, the over-powered enderman, and of course the written book. All of the responses to my post left me downhearted. Not one person who replied had experienced these things. They all seemed to agree that my game was being hacked. So I took my case to customer support. I gave them my computer's specs, and they began their investigation. A week had passed before they gave a response back. They couldn't find anything wrong with my game. According to them, there was nothing wrong with the code or anything. I huffed a little. I was stuck with what I had.

My morning was spent wandering aimlessly around my house waiting for the sand to smelt into glass. I glanced at Growls, and he cocked his head. I went to the chest to fetch him some food. I was getting a little low on meat, but there was plenty of rotten flesh. It felt weird giving it to him, but it would have to do for now. Growls ate it and sat by the bed, tail up in contentment. I checked on the sand in the furnace, and it was about halfway through the stack. I took what was finished and placed it in my inventory. I needed to kill time so I tended to the garden. All the crops were doing very well. It seems like there was always a surplus of vegetables now. I harvested each row and was heading back inside when a sudden, familiar flash of teal caught my eye.

It was very hard to make out, but it looked like a person in the distance. It was the shirt of a zombie that caught my eye. No, wait, that wasn't right. It was out in the sunlight, and its skin wasn't that nauseating green. This was a player. But I was in my single player world, right? I tried to squint and see if there was a name above its head. The fog made it impossible to make anything out. As soon as I blinked, the figure disappeared. What was going on with my game? Or was there something wrong with me? Maybe that was it. After all, I had mistaken plants for creepers before out of my peripheries. Yeah, that was probably the case.

I went back inside and stored my
vegetables. I checked my furnace, and all my
glass was made. The sun was beginning to set
so my renovations had to wait until morning. I
went to sleep with Growls by my side. When I
woke up I noticed Growls was not where I had
left him. I walked around the corner and saw
the dog staring outside the front window. I
tried to get him to sit down, but he wouldn't
respond. I offered some chicken to him, but he
wouldn't take it. Was he stuck? I tried to push
him away from the window, but he would go
right back to it. He didn't even make a sound.
He was transfixed on the window. Finally I
peered out the window to see what had his

attention. He was looking toward the forest. Stepping outside revealed something bizarre to me.

Those were the saplings I had planted earlier. They were left alone to grow into large, tall trees. But now I could see that some had lost all their leaves. They couldn't have just fallen off. There weren't any saplings on the ground either. Another glitch, I suspected. This was starting to get annoying. I decided to chop down the bare tree trunks. They weren't very pleasing to look at. Luckily I had some more saplings with me, and I planted them as replacements. I was just about to plant the last one when I saw a spider lunge at me from a few blocks above. I practically jumped out of my skin. In my panic, I didn't even bother switching to my sword. The spider was bludgeoned repeatedly with an oak sapling. I let out a deep sigh once it disappeared in a small plume of smoke, leaving nothing behind but some spider silk on the ground. I picked that up and made my way back home before I had any more surprises.

I returned home and noticed Growls had made his way back to my bedside as if he never moved from that spot. I eyed him suspiciously, and he cocked his head in response. I rolled my eyes and brought him some rotten flesh from the chest. No use fretting about his strange behavior. It's all the work of some hacker anyway, I thought. I started breaking down the wooden blocks of my roof and put a glass block in their place. The moon was beginning to rise and not much progress had been made. I frowned, but I had to call it a night. I didn't want to take the risk of letting some monster in while I put holes in my roof.

The night came and went in an instant. When I woke, Growls had once again left my bedside. I found the dog looking out the side window toward the small beach. I scanned the area to see what other anomaly had taken place in my game.

It was that player again. He was replacing the sand I had dug up from the beach. Growls and I watched him place each block of sand with careful precision. It was as if he knew exactly where each block should go. He made it look like I never even touched that beach, and it boggled my mind. Why would he do this? Could he be trying to mess with my mind? That's when everything clicked. This was the hacker. He's come into my game to straight-up troll me. I wanted badly to confront the guy, but I had no idea how to approach him. I was sure that if I attacked him, he would break my game. However the chat window was useless in single-player mode. I was searching through my options when it hit me. I would write in a book and give it to him.

things normal again. I hooked around back to my house.

The coldest chill made its way up my spine. I was now face to face with the hacker. He had not left me. His appearance mirrored mine only his eyes were eerily whited-out. I stared into those eyes for what felt like an eternity. There was such force behind that stare that the ground shook beneath me. No. That was me trembling. I had to wonder what he saw as his gaze bore right through me. It felt like he was gazing at more than just my character. He was looking fixedly at Steve. My body could not be willed to move. Then, my screen spontaneously flashed. When my eyes adjusted, the hacker was gone, and my game told me I had died. I respawned back in bed, trying to figure out what just happened. I stood there in a daze for a bit until I took note of something floating at the end of my bed. It was a book. I picked and delicately opened it. Inside, the words were a mess of pixels. Only a few sentences were legible.

You are not worthy.
Not yet.
What is the game you are playing?
You don't even know.
If you want to see this to the end,
You will follow.

I think I'm beginning to understand what this guy wants. He wants to play some twisted game with me. If I oblige him, would he be satisfied and leave me alone? There is no way of knowing what would happen. But I will stick by my words. He won't stop me from doing what I love. Fine, I will follow you. Whatever it is that you'll have me do, I will persevere. I said once before that I am the hero of this world. I suppose I'm no hero without my own villain, huh? At least I'm not alone. If it weren't for Growls, the chance to meet this guy would have slipped right passed me. I wonder who he really is and what he's all about. Why did he choose my game? Maybe the answers will reach me in time. For now, I've got a new nemesis to engage.

Book Two: The Unfinished Game

My name is Steve, and I guess I'm the hero of this world. Actually, I haven't been feeling very heroic lately. I mean, I defeat monsters on a daily basis, and I've acquired an arch nemesis, so I suppose that constitutes as being a hero. But lately, I'm beginning to question whether or not my actions truly matter. Like what difference does it make how many zombies I kill? There will always be more tomorrow. Why do I keep rebuilding my house when endermen and creepers will come and tear it apart? Why do I seek out diamonds when they too will break in the end? I'm sorry. I'm getting a little ahead of myself. Let me go back and explain how I got to this point.

As I mentioned, I have found myself a nemesis. He's a hacker who has come into my single-player game for reasons I don't know. He's been tampering around with the game's code, causing unusual things to happen. He likes to observe how I react to such events. He's always watching me with pure white eyes. If it weren't for those soul-piercing eyes, I would've swore I was looking in the mirror. He has begun to prepare all sorts of trials for me, all of which are not very straightforward. If he's feeling generous, he'll toss a written book my way. These usually contain some vague and almost unreadable hint. Unfortunately this is the limit of our communication. I can sense he's holding back a lot of information, but the only way I'm going to squeeze it out of him is if I do what he wants, much to my annoyance.

The first of the hacker's trials began when I was navigating my way out of a cave after a supply run for iron and coal. In an instant, he removed all the torches in my inventory as well as the ones I had placed around the cave. I instantly knew what blindness felt like. It was so dark that I couldn't even see my hand in front of my face. To make things worse, the moans and clinks of zombies and skeletons were all around me, but I had no clue where they were. My heart was racing. My only thought was to go up. That's how I'd get out of there. I managed to feel my way through while continuously jumping and wildly swinging my sword. My sword collided with several zombies and skeletons. Their pained cries were my only comfort in the pitch blackness. For ten minutes I bounced around in the dark, praying that progress was being made. My prayers were answered, and I saw a glimmer of light from above. I frantically hopped toward it.

Before I knew it I was out in the daylight again. I have never been so thankful to see the sun. That really did a number on my nerves. As

I was pulling myself together, a shadow loomed over me. I peered up to see it was my hacker. He stared at me intensely. I can never bring myself to look away from him as I do with the endermen. While an enderman's stare is haunting, my hacker's stare was just plain unreadable. It was neither good nor bad. It had no alignment. But its power shook me to the core. The stare was brief this time. He turned his head to the side and teleported away. I assumed that meant I had passed his first test. That's one victory point for Steve.

The second test didn't come until a week later. In the meantime, I had finished changing the roof to my house. The old homestead had been given some upgrades over time. The roof had been replaced with glass for easy spider-detection. Also, it now had two floors. The first floor had a living room, an armory and a kitchen. The top floor contained my bedroom, a library and a small pen for my dog, Growls. At the end of the week, I checked my kitchen chest for some dinner for my canine companion. I was shocked to find only one pork chop left in the entire chest. My brow furrowed. I was getting hungry too. I went to my armory and fetched my diamond sword. It was time to go for a hunt.

I stepped out the front door and surveyed my garden. There were some carrots almost ready for harvest. I figured I'd save those for myself while I got Growls some meat. I cut a path through the nearby forest until I sighted a herd of cows. There were six of them staying idle around a patch of poppies. My eyes locked on to the nearest cow. I sprinted up behind it and slashed it hastily. It never stood a chance. Some leather and two pieces of beef were now mine. I started plucking off cows from the herd one by one until only two remained. I gathered the rest of the leather and beef scattering the ground. The two cows left behind would become the first of a new herd. They had sampled some of my wheat, and I gave them space to repopulate. Whatever I took from this world, I would try to give back. It's just who I was. I hummed happily back to my abode. Growls and I would be eating well tonight, I thought. It wasn't until I reached the clearing that I found that my hacker had other plans.

My garden had been bathed in vibrant flames. I clambered toward my home, desperately trying to put out the fires. The inferno was stopped before it encompassed my home, luckily. But the damage had already been done. My fence had some minor gaps in it, but my garden was completely obliterated. Only my rows of water had defended against the fire. I had to put my discouragement aside. The fence needed to be repaired pronto. I withdrew my leftover fencing from my chest and swiftly rebuilt my fence. Now there was at least some protection surrounding me. Sadness encircled me as I cooked my beef. There weren't any seeds in my chest. I'd have to start the garden over from scratch. Growls was given his piece of the hunt while I flopped lazily into bed.

I was filled with a new sense of purpose at daybreak. Today, I'd hunt for seeds. Leaving the house, I couldn't help but take in my barren fields. It was a loss, yes, but did my hacker seriously think putting a torch to everything would stop me from rebuilding? Please. I strolled up to my gate and tried to open it. It stayed closed. I clicked it again and again, but it held firm. I sighed. My hacker. I did a U-turn back to my house and retrieved my axe. I faced the fence and swung my axe in a concentrated frenzy. The fence post never even cracked after a solid minute of hacking and slashing. Okay, I thought, time for plan B. Back inside the house again, I withdrew some dirt blocks from the chest. If I can't go through it, I'll go over it. Facing the fence once more, I tried to place a dirt block in front of me. My arm went through the motion of placing the block, but it never left my hand. My predicament had finally become clear. Feelings of being trapped had surfaced within me. This was my hacker's true intent. I was to live as a prisoner in my own home.

The seriousness of my situation intensified as my hunger grew. With the garden gone, my only food sources were the lone pork chop and the six pieces of steak from the hunt. This didn't leave much considering Growls needed to eat too. I divided the steak between us over the next couple of days. Time passed painfully slow. I thought of all the days that kept me busy with tasks that seemed so trivial. I had become aware of how important they were to my sanity. Now, my only project was to watch the sun rise and fall.

After three days of keeping Growls and myself full, all that remained was that one pork chop. My hunger meter has fallen considerably, and I had to make a choice. Growls wasn't doing much better. His tail hung low, and he looked at me with pleading eyes.

It was between me and him. Thoughts came pouring into my head. He isn't even a real dog so why should I bother feeding him? Then again I didn't really count as real either because I was just a pixelated character, so why should I have to feed myself and not him? Well, if my hunger meter fell to zero and I died, I could always respawn back to my bed. But what if I didn't respawn? Could the hacker do that? If he was capable of preventing me from leaving my home, it seemed pretty logical to assume he could keep me from respawning. I now felt paranoia creeping up on me. The weight of this decision had just revealed itself. Who gets to live another day—me or my faithful companion?

I had to admit that despite this being a game, I really did feel a connection to Growls. He's saved me from monsters more times than I could count. My mind immediately flashed back to that lone enderman. I made the error of looking it in the eye and knew I would pay the price. It whittled my health down to the point of no return, and I thought for sure I was done for. But Growls had come to my rescue, and I was forever grateful that I had him. My mind was made up.

Growls' tail perked up as he devoured the pork chop and hearts had flowered around him. My choice was the right one. I watched my health dwindle away and awaited my end. I died with no regrets and respawned back in my bed. I had grown paranoid for nothing and my nerves finally relaxed. Now I had to ponder my next course of action. There was no food for either of us now. Was I going to be stuck in a cycle of starvation and death?

As I contemplated my options, I noticed Growls walk over to front window. I immediately followed him, and sure enough, there was my hacker standing outside the window. His eyes connected with mine through the glass. His eyes still disturbed me, but I was able to hold a firm stance against him. The fear was there, but I was able to grasp it and hold it still. He gradually turned his head toward the gate of my fence, and stared at it with mild interest. He then returned my gaze and teleported away. After a second of processing this exchange I sprang from my house and rushed toward the gate. I hesitated slightly . . . then clicked. The gate unbarred with a pop that was music to my ears.

A month passed, and my garden was reborn. Growls and I were no longer in shortage of food; we were flourishing. Just a day ago I went to the local village and traded some emeralds for pieces of watermelon. I crafted them into seeds and spread them through the garden. I was so thrilled to have a new crop to my fields. If I were to go hungry, it would be my own fault.

As I finished my harvest for the day, I was growing concerned at the lack of my dear villain's appearance. What could he have been plotting for me now? Once everything was safely sealed in my chest, I decided I'd seek him out myself. I began my search south of my home's clearing. Sprawling plains made way for a large swamp. I bobbed and weaved through vines and lily pads. I surveyed the entire marsh for any sign of my mysterious guest. In the distance, a barely visible witch stood motionless on an island. I could make out a shadow next to her. It had to be him. Consorting with witches was totally his style. I was careful with my approach. Startling a witch had never resulted in anything good.

I was trying my best to be stealthy as I crouched among a herd of pigs. I regretted this idea immediately as there was this one pig that wouldn't get out of my way. I tried to move forward, but it just kept pacing in front of me. I was completely fed up with its antics. With sword in hand, I slew it where it stood. I collected the raw pork it dropped and continued my advance toward the witch. I was close enough now to that my suspicions were correct. There was my hacker, his gaze directed at the witch. Strangely, he never looked upon me as he usually does. That piercing gaze remained on the witch for a mere moment before he faded out of the swamp. As soon as he was gone, the witch instantly spun around.

She flung a potion whose contents spilled all over me. The potion seemed to make me shrink in size. I prepared for another bottled assault, but the witch halted her attack. This gave me time to put myself on the offense. I tried to switch to my sword but it had disappeared from my inventory. In fact all of my items were gone. I glared up at the witch and in pure anger I tried to attack her with my bare hands. I gasped in horror to see that my hands had vanished as well. What did she do to me? I switched my view to the third person and was completely baffled. Instead of viewing my human self, I saw something pink and pudgy with this vacant expression. I had been turned into a pig.

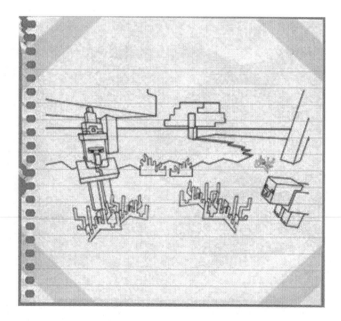

I gawked at the witch in astonishment. Potions like this only existed in mods of the game. My white-eyed nemesis had struck again. In a feeble attempt at communication, I hopped and skipped around the witch hoping she would change me back. She wouldn't even look at me. This was getting me nowhere. The one I really had to find was my hacker. Finding him, though, would be like finding a creeper in a forest. I trudged through the swamp back to my clearing. It occurred to me as I neared my fence, that I had no hands to open the gate. I was also too short to jump over it. I couldn't go home.

I paced around outside my fence trying to think of where my hacker would go. The abandoned house in the forest drifted to my mind. It was the best place to start. I hobbled through the woods. My inability to run was becoming more and more bothersome. I moved in on the roofless shack. With the exception of the large gaping hole in the front, courtesy of a creeper, there was nothing out of the ordinary about the old hut. I snorted sadly and shuffled my way back through the forest. A low, sinister growl snapped me from my thoughts. I knew there was a pack of wolves in these woods, but I paid them no mind. That growl, though, was unusual. That was the one they used when attacking. Whirling around, I was met with five pairs of blood-red eyes. They all were fixated on me. What did I do? I can't attack anybody. My eyes widened, and my heart stopped. I was a pig. Were they really going to them made any advances toward me. There was no aggression in their behavior. These beings used to fill me with nothing but dread. Right now though, I felt sheltered.

Throughout the night, things I never thought of before had crept their way into my head. Could this be the reason these guys attack me every night? Were they trying to protect the animals I hunted? Guilt had taken root inside my heart. I thought of the pig I had butchered earlier. It didn't deserve that. As a human, I believed the pigs here lived a carefree life. I was very wrong. A pig's vulnerability had been shown to me. If it weren't for these normally hostile mobs, the pigs would all have been slaughtered by wolves or, worse, an ignorant human like me.

The sun had begun to rise. The creeper and spiders had wandered off to their little alcoves. The zombies and skeletons hung around in a trance. The sun's rays bore down on the undead and plumes of fire engulfed them. They wailed out in pain, and my heart broke. I desperately wanted to lead them to the shade of forest trees, but I couldn't get close to them without catching fire myself. I was forced to watch my newfound saviors burn to their deaths. Tears began to flood my eyes. Who would have thought I'd grieve for these creatures. Bones and rotten flesh floated gently above the ground. These items I would hoard without question now made my stomach churn. I sat there debating what I should do with these remains, when teal caught my eye.

The white-eyed hacker stood over one depressed little pig. I gazed up into his expressionless face. I was too distraught to have any kind of fear for his haunting view. He crouched down to my level and slowly placed his hand on my head. This left me dumbfounded. I had not thought him capable of sympathy. He stood up and took a few steps back. A glimmering potion bottle materialized in his hand. He threw the bottle at me with splash. I watched in amazement as I grew to eye-level with him. I looked down to see my arms had returned. I was also able to open my inventory and was delighted to see all of my items were there. I closed my inventory to see my hacker had taken his leave. My perception of him as a villain was beginning to falter. There had to be a point to all this. I couldn't fathom what. I believe it was about time he and I had a real heart-to-heart. Er, well, book-to-book. But that would have to wait. For now, I was just grateful to be human again.

I entered my home and recoiled in fright. One of those rabid wolves made its way into my house. Oh wait, it was just Growls. I sighed deeply. Being a pig had taken its toll on me. I vowed to never eat another pork chop again. But bread was still on the menu, and my plight as a pig left me starving. Using the wheat from my inventory, I crafted three loaves and feasted. With my hunger bar completely full, I exited the homestead. From my front porch I could recognize a familiar floating item by the fence gate. One of my hacker's written books. I flipped through its pages searching for some less jumbled text I could read. I found a few sentences.

Do you know why Ghasts cry?
They weep for the ones fate abandoned.
Hear their restless decay.
Make them sleep.

Hmm. I never really thought about why the ghast cries. I thought that was just how it was made. According to my hacker, they were crying over someone. If I wanted to find out whom, I knew where I had to go. A place I would have liked to forget. A realm filled with demons and the souls of the damned. The nether. I had traveled there once before to sate my curiosity. Never had I been so unsettled by my environment. One thing rang truly and clearly when I entered the fiery domain: I did not belong there. I relished the thought of having to return to that burning wasteland. Did I really have to go back there? What would happen if I didn't? I came to the conclusion that there was more behind my hacker's tests than just watching me flounder about in confusion. There was something in the nether he wanted me to see. I might as well indulge him, I thought.

I entered my armory and gazed upon the set of diamond armor I had mounted on the wall. That set would definitely be needed. I suited up and made my way into the kitchen. I prepared some more food including cookies and pumpkin pie. Growls sat in the living and barked to get my attention. I looked down at my ever faithful companion. As much as I wanted to take him with me, I knew he would not last long. He probably wouldn't even make it to the nether portal. You see, I built that portal at the bottom of a deep ravine, the top of which was barred with dirt blocks. I had heard rumors that those hellish fiends could make their way through the portal into my plain. There was no way I'd let them run free on my terrain.

Once my gear felt sufficient, I traveled to the ravine. I carefully navigated my way down, using cobblestone blocks I gathered along the way as makeshift stairs. I stood in front of the portal, hypnotized by its swirling purple vortexes and its gurgling, infernal screeches. Even the mere entrance to this place reeked of evil. I gulped slightly, and sweat formed in my palms. A countdown began in my head. Three, two, one. I threw myself into the portal. The vortexes danced around me transporting me far away from my comforts. My vision faded into the violet swirls. After a brief moment of blindness I emerged from the portal into the accursed dimension.

I had spawned in a small, empty cave. The netherrack that encompassed me had its signature color and grit that resembled dried blood. I hiked toward the cave entrance that was completely sealed off by a wall of glass. Now why was that there? Did my hacker suddenly have a concern for my safety? I doubted it. I started to approach the glass but immediately froze mid-step. On the other side of the wall were hundreds of wither skeletons. They had pressed themselves against the wall, their lifeless eyes locked on mine. The familiar clink of their bones was drowned out by another noise I had never heard before. It was like a murmur or whisper. As I edged closer to the wall, the voices became louder and clearer. They spoke rapidly without pause for breath.

*IPLAYEDTHEGAMEIPLAYEDTHEG
AMEIPLAYEDTHEGAME.
ILOSTTHEGAMEILOSTTHEGAMEIL
OSTTHEGAME.
ITRIEDTODEFYITITRIEDTODEFYITIT
RIEDTODEFYIT.
WHATMADEMEMORTALWHATMAD
EMEMORTALWHATMADEMEMORTAL.
NOWISUFFERNOWISUFFERNOWISU
FFERNOWISUFFER.
ENDENDENDENDENDENDENDEN
DENDENDENDENDEND.*

I covered my ears with my hands and backed away from the wall. Their collective voices were deafening. Their words put my hair on edge and my heart pounded in my chest. I couldn't listen to them any longer. I was about to turn and run when the shattering of glass stopped me in my tracks. The withers raised their swords, smashing the glass wall block by block.

I gaped in horror as they swarmed into the cave, their speech growing ever louder and quicker. I tried to clamber my way to the portal, but the skeletons blocked it off. They had me surrounded in seconds. Trembling, I drew my sword. This was my only way out. They came at me, their bones clanging heavily. My sword swung at them in frenzied slashes. When there was a gap in the crowd I dove through it, putting some distance between the mob and myself. I positioned myself to take them on in a straight line. One by one the withered skeletons crumpled to the floor. I dodged and countered their attacks until finally I stood alone in a sea of bones. Exhausted, I stumbled through the portal and fell onto the earth.

This ordeal was what made me question my status as a hero. Did I just fight monsters or forsaken souls? Could I have done something to save them? What I had just witnessed was beyond some game. This was not something a mere hacker could achieve. Good lord, those voices echoed in my mind. Wanting to get as far away from that portal as possible, I swiftly climbed out of the ravine and headed home. I stood in my living room, lost in thought, munching on a cookie. When my meal was finished, I grabbed one of my books from the chest. I opened it and stared at the blank page. I had wanted to write down all of my questions and concerns for my next encounter with the hacker, but the sentences wouldn't form properly in my head. I grumbled and closed the book. As I did so, I noticed an empty slot in my inventory had been filled. Inside, were three skulls from the wither skeletons. I didn't even realize I had picked them up.

As I stared into the face of the decaying skull, its words once again reverberated in me. They had played a game and lost. A feeling I know all too well. But why did they have to suffer? Losing a game didn't warrant such a cruel punishment, right? I saw in the skull a kindred spirit. These were who the ghasts pity so. And I didn't blame them. I certainly would cry for tormented souls. Crying isn't enough, though. Some action had to be taken. I knew there was little I could do, but for my own peace of mind, I had to do something.

I marched through the clearing and onto a hill. A single birch tree was perched on the top. At its roots, I dug three holes, each two blocks down. I placed a skull in each hole and covered the top with dirt. I marked each hole with a stone slab and surveyed my handiwork. A simple grave was the least I could give them. I prayed they would be able to rest. I glanced to my left. My hacker was praying too. I stared him down, and he gradually returned my gaze. His blank eyes reminded me of the empty pages of the book in my hand. With him in my sights, all I had wanted to say was able to flow from my mind to the paper.

You're not really a hacker, are you?
What just happened was beyond simply tampering with code.
Who are you?
What kind of game are you playing with me?
I know there's something you want me to understand.
Every test you gave me was to teach me something about myself.
Bravery, selflessness, perspective, empathy
They all are leading to something else, right?
So just tell me.
Please.
-Steve

I casually tossed him the book. He picked it up and held it for a moment or two, then threw it back to me. I flipped the book open, surprised to see that there were no jumbles of pixels. The message was perfectly clear.

You now have worth.
There is one thing left to do.
It will all become clear in the end.
- Herobrine

You now have worth.

There is one thing left to do.

It will all become clear in the end.

- Herobrine

Book Three: The Endings and Beginnings of a Legend

My name is Steve, and I am no hero. I'm just a guy trying to figure things out. For a while now, I had been dealing with what I thought was a hacker in my single-player game. In recent events, he had shown me that he was no hacker. I didn't know exactly what he was, but I had his name. Herobrine. Herobrine was trying to show me something within the game. He had made me go through different scenarios in order to prove my "worth." Fumbling in the dark, starving to death, living as a pig, putting the departed to rest—I did it all. I was considered worthy now, but there was one last hurdle to jump through.

Herobrine and I communicated through written books in the game. His last note told me everything would become clear in the end. I puzzled over what "end" he could've meant. The answer hit me in the middle of the night. It was a tiring day, and I was ready to retire for the night. I went up to the second floor of my home with my dog, Growls, right behind me. I yelped in surprise to see an enderman had teleported its way into my home. I glanced outside and understood. It was seeking shelter from the rain.

Throughout my journeys, I've encountered many mobs and learned their stories. The endermen, however, were always wrapped in mystery. I assumed their only purpose was to move blocks around and scare the ever living sense out of me if I looked at them. With all that had happened, I wondered if that was really true. In any case, there was no way I was going to sleep soundly with one in my house. I readied Growls and drew my sword. My sword sliced its legs, while Growls nipped at its feet. We had it down before it could even teleport.

Our fantastic teamwork had rewarded Growls and me . . . an eye of ender? Wasn't this supposed to be an ender pearl? Were eyes of ender rare drops now? I wasn't going to question it further. Stranger things had happened. I filed through my memory bank, trying to recall what the eyes were used for. I had it. They were used to make a special kind of portal. One that led to the enderman's home world: The End. OH. My mind flashed back to the note where I first learned Herobrine's name. I had worth now and everything would become clear in the end. But not just any end, The End. That had to be what he meant. He wanted me to go there. But exactly how was a blur to me. I was too tired to think it through. I'd worry about it in the morning.

I awoke at dawn to find Herobrine at the edge of my bed. His pure white eyes had once terrified me, but now they just filled me with questions. At one time I had called him my nemesis. Someone who was out to taunt and torture me. But my view since then had changed. I couldn't exactly call him a friend, but neither could I call him an enemy. I had to settle with calling him my guide. My guide to the unknown. He turned and walked out of my home, his moves slow and precise as usual. Seeing him walk instead of using his typical teleportation skills had caught my interest. I was to follow him.

Herobrine led me through the clearing and into the nearby forest. We made our way to the abandoned shack. Now that I thought about it, this was where everything started. The roofless, wooden hut had been the first of many strange occurrences in my game. Its design was that of something a player had built and ditched halfway through the job. I certainly hadn't built it. It must have been Herobrine. I watched him marvel at the house as if struck by some fond memory. He walked over to where the chest that contained the very first written book had been. I vaguely remembered its contents. Some player was haunted by a mysterious entity who had rewritten the rules of the game. It sounded an awful lot like Herobrine. So I wasn't the only one to encounter him.

Herobrine stood where the chest had been. In a single swipe of his hand, the wooden block broke, revealing a ladder beneath it. With a quick glance at me he hopped down the hole. I peered down the single-block passage. It went deep into the darkness. I gulped and hesitantly grabbed hold of the ladder. I carefully made my way down. The hole seemed like it would go on into the center of the earth. After a few minutes of climbing straight down, I could make out some light below me. I jumped off the ladder with a thud. I inspected my surrounding to find I had landed in a stone-brick hallway.

Herobrine waited for me at the end of it. I ran to catch up to him. I followed him down several corridors connected with iron doors. This had to be one of those strongholds I had heard about. If that was the case, then I knew where Herobrine was taking me. But, shouldn't there have been monsters about? It was eerily quiet down here. I wasn't sure if Herobrine kept them away or if he had dealt with them personally. Either way my instinct was to keep my guard up. Herobrine led me into a dimly lit room. In the center were some stairs that gave way to the makings of what would be a portal.

Blocks I've never seen before floated in a square above a pool of lava. Each block had an indentation, some of which were filled with eyes of ender. I took the eye I had acquired earlier and placed it gingerly in one of the slots. That left seven more to fill, and then I would be able to reach The End. I faced Herobrine and nodded. In his hand was a book. He tossed it my way, and I caught it with ease. I flipped it open.

Seven remain.
Enders wander the world.
Their masters will relinquish their eyes.
The first is frozen in time.
Crystalized in its apathy.
Go.

I closed the book to find myself alone. So there are special endermen that drop eyes instead of pearls. I had to wonder; couldn't I just kill the regular endermen, take their pearls and craft the eyes of ender? Ah, but crafting the eyes required some powder from the blazes in the nether. I had no desire to return there any time soon. The droning voices of the wither skeletons continued to haunt me to this day. I would take my chances with these "masters" of the endermen.

I speculated where this first enderman could be. Frozen in time, crystalized in its apathy. The most logical choice would be somewhere cold, I figured. My mind displayed images of the small beach to the east of my house. I could've sworn there was a snowy plain across the sea from there. It was good place to start. I climbed up and out of the stronghold and dashed through the woods toward home. First things first, I needed a boat. I placed some oak blocks on the crafting table and converted them to wooden planks. I then placed the wooden planks in a U formation on the table, and I had my boat. I made for the beach with Growls in tow. I knew I would need him if I was going to deal with some nasty endermen.

I trekked out to the small beach that scanned the horizon. I could make out some snowy land in the distance. I set the boat down and hopped in. I reacquainted myself with its controls and steered straight ahead. I watched the waves rush past me as I sailed. Soon white specks brushed into my face. I looked toward the sky with a smile. It's been a while since I had seen snow. It was sort of difficult to see, but it had a calming effect on me. I slowed the boat down and sidled it up to the snow-dusted beach. I jumped out and placed the boat in my inventory before it had a chance to float away. I waited patiently for Growls, who had been swimming behind. He climbed the shore and casually shook himself dry. We then journeyed into the frosted meadow.

My feet crunched softly with each step in the powder. After traveling through the endless white, Growls and I reached the top of a small hill. What we saw dazzled us. Thousands of ice spires breached through the earth toward the sky. Some were so tall they kissed the clouds. They twinkled in the daylight and had me mesmerized. We wandered among the spikes, taking in their otherworldly beauty. I felt that I was literally in a land frozen in time. I shook my head. I couldn't let the artistry of this place distract me. I had to find this special enderman. How I would be able to tell it apart from regular endermen left me perplexed. I guessed I'd know it when I saw it.

Growls and I roamed through the icy land until we saw the cold spikes give way for a frozen pond. In the center stood an enderman holding a block of packed ice. A block which I knew endermen shouldn't have been able to pick up. This was the enderman I was to hunt, for sure. I unsheathed my sword and dauntlessly stared at its face. Yet it didn't even flinch. In fact, it made no movements at all. If I didn't know better, I'd believe it was statue. I inched a bit closer and glared into its eyes. Nothing. Its stillness made me nervous. Was it truly frozen? I raised my sword to strike it when a snarl broke out of Growls. I glanced over my shoulder to see what aggravated him.

Snow Golems were emerging from the meadows. They congregated around the iced-covered pond, surrounding us. These constructible snowmen were normally peaceful beings. They often allied themselves with their creators and served as a layer of defense by pelting nearby foes with snowballs. The way they encircled us now was a clear sign of attack. That could only mean they came to protect their master. This enderman had built them. I raised up my sword to cover my face as the snowballs began flying. I could hear Growls viciously attacking the golems as I struggled to withstand their onslaught. When there was a break in the action, I sprung forward cutting them down one by one. I was lucky the golems didn't have much health, but there sure were a lot of them. Growls and I assailed the snowmen evading their projectiles as best we could. My sword had to become my shield as I deflected the snowballs being thrown like cannon fire. While I stayed on the defense, Growls had kept up his offense. The snow golems were unable to resist his bite, and it wasn't long until the two of us stood panting in an ocean of snowballs.

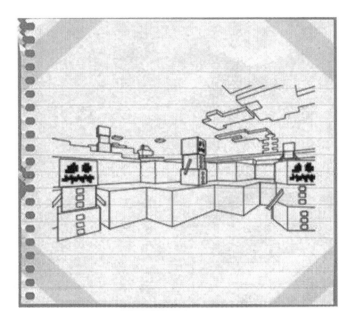

I caught my breath and peered at the petrified enderman. Its head had moved to gape at me. However, it remained unprovoked. It appeared there was nothing I could do to upset it. Not even the destruction of its creations would light a fire within it. Without breaking any eye contact I rent its legs until it fell. It dissolved into the snow leaving an eye of ender in its place. I scooped it up with a sense of pride. One down, six more to go. Growls and I trudged back to the frozen shore. As we approached I could make out a person overlooking the sea. Herobrine. I ran to meet him. He turned, looking me over. When he felt I met his approval he casted another book at my feet and beamed away. I snatched it and read.

> *The second hides itself in the undergrowth.*
> *Ashamed of what it doesn't have.*
> *Cut off its wanting ways.*

Undergrowth, eh? There's plenty of it in a jungle. I knew the forest near home was a passageway to one. I prepared my boat and sailed back to my clearing. I stopped at home to deposit all the snowballs I'd collected and moved on. As I approached the forest, I could see the jungle canopy loom behind it. I had to be wary. There were plenty of hiding places in that dense foliage. I cut my way through in determination. The jungle emerged like a giant monster's maw. It had a presence all its own. Leaf blocks had covered its floor like a blanket. I doubted I ever touched the earth as I traveled inward.

I kept my eye all around me. An ambush could occur at any moment. Scanning the canopy, I could hear faint, gurgling noises. I followed the sounds until I could identify them. They were indeed an enderman's warbles. The noise was so audible I felt like I was standing right on top of the creature, but it remained hidden from me. Focusing my hearing, I tried to pinpoint its exact location. Aiming myself toward one particular tree, I began to scrutinize it. The enderman was there. It was using its height to mimic part of the tree trunk. Very clever. I advanced toward the shadowy being, sword drawn back. I stared it in the face, issuing my challenge.

The enderman stared right back at me, unperturbed by my gaze. It looked me up and down, assessing me. When it had finished, it sauntered over to me and plucked the diamond sword from my hand. I gaped in astonishment as it marveled at the weapon. It suddenly snapped its head back to me, and its jaw unhinged in a silent battle cry. The enderman thrust the sword in my face forcing me to jump back. With my weapon gone, I had to use the next best thing. I drew my axe and hacked away at it. Growls gnawed on its legs but was tossed back by the force of the swinging sword. With its attention on Growls, I sprung behind it and came down with one, powerful chop. It dropped my sword and spun around. As the enderman tried to reach for the sword, Growls rushed in front of it and dealt the final blow. Good dog.

With the second eye of ender secured, I traipsed through the jungle, back toward home. Glancing down at my recovered sword, I puzzled over why the enderman would want it. It seemed rather envious and frankly, who wouldn't be? Diamond is an ore found purely by chance. It's something you could acquire only with the right tools and skills. I could understand how the enderman felt as I recollected back to my days using nothing but wooden equipment. Diamond was nothing but a distant dream back then.

I entered the clearing where a spot of red caught my eye. A patch of rose bushes had formed in the normally flowerless field. Nestled in the middle of them was an enderman holding a poppy. Could this be another "master"? Walking over to it had immediately alerted it to my presence. The enderman teleported from the rose bushes to in front of me. It looked at me, but like the others, there was no sign of aggression. It held the poppy out to me. I stepped back a few paces. It also moved a few paces, keeping the same distance between us. It continued to hold out the poppy. I think it wanted me to take it, but I had no idea if this was a trap or an offering of friendship. Those violet eyes that made tremble in fear so many times prevented me from trusting it. I shook my head no. It suddenly got even closer, putting the poppy right in my face. Again, I shook my head no.

Now the enderman was enraged. It threw the poppy on the ground and came at me, mouth agape. I swiped at it with my sword, but it teleported behind me before I could make the hit. It knocked off a good portion of my health, and I went in for the counter. Growls and I performed a double attack pushing the enderman back. We continued our barrage of attacks until it fell to the ground with a dying scream. An eye of ender formed in its resting spot. Now that the deed was done, I could only begin to imagine what would have happened if I accepted the poppy. Would it have attacked me anyway? My shoulders slumped. These peculiar endermen were exhausting me. I ate a loaf of bread and retired to my home. As soon as the sun set, I hit the bed.

In the morning, a new book had been left in my living room. I packed away a few more loaves of bread form the kitchen and went to pick it up. It was, of course, from Herobrine. I opened it anxiously, curious to see who was next on my hit list.

The fourth and fifth have a lot in common.
They take and take and never give back.
They are a plague to those around them.
Eliminate them.

So I'll be tackling two endermen at once this time. I checked my gear to make sure I was suitable for this task. Everything seemed to be in order. The note made it feel like these two endermen were in a crowded place. The only place I could imagine was a village. This was good. I had planned to stop at the one nearby to trade a few things anyway. Growls and I hiked over the plains to where the village lay. When we reached the outskirts, we saw an enderman that seemed to be guarding one of the village's farms. Upon closer inspection, the enderman had closed off the farm and was surrounded by cake that it was devouring one after the other.

It appeared that this enderman had cut off the village's food supply to feed itself. I watched in disgust as it gorged itself on the surrounding cake. This couldn't go on any longer. I ran straight for the monster and plunged my sword into its stomach. It cried out in pain and teleported to the center of the village. Growls and I chased it down and launched a flurry of quick attacks. Just when I thought it was about to go down, it gave out this otherworldly yell that I've never heard before. The sound brought my attacks to a grinding halt. Looking at the creature in confusion, I almost didn't hear the sound of a teleporting enderman behind me.

I spun around and sure enough, the second enderman had shown itself. In its hands it a held a block of solid emerald that it seemed very unwilling to give up. While the first enderman had robbed the village of its food, this enderman had taken their currency. This pair was downright despicable. The enderman with the emerald flew at me, while the other one focused on Growls. The battle commenced until they had sandwiched us against the town forge. In a burst of agility, I parried around them and dispatched the first enderman. The emerald-carrying enderman shook with fury and lunged after me. I blocked with my sword as Growls maimed it from behind. In one, last arc of my sword, the enderman dropped to the ground. I pocketed the two eyes of ender and saw the villagers emerge from their houses, grunting excitedly. Life here was back to normal.

Unlike the previous endermen I had slain, this pair of endermen did not evoke any feelings of remorse. What they did to the village was wrong. But then again there have been circumstances when I would take from others and not give back. When I first entered this world, I hoarded everything I could find. I charged through the wilderness like a natural disaster. I think it was when I found my first diamond that I had a change of heart. I had found what I desired, so there really wasn't a need to keep everything for myself. And once I had started giving back to the world, I felt like a better person.

I made my way back to the village outskirts and saw Herobrine waiting for me. He gave me a small nod of approval. Everything was going well. He once again chucked a book at my feet. I studied the note.

The sixth has climbed its way to the top.
It will not move for anything beneath it.
You'll be rid of it quickly, but be careful.
The seventh lurks nearby.
It will avenge its comrades.

This one I didn't have to think hard about. There was a tall mountain that I had been mining the base out of. The tip of it had penetrated through the clouds and beyond. After all of my travels, this one was the highest mountain I had come across. I had no doubt in my mind I would find the enderman there. I helped myself to some of the leftover cake in the village and seized raw chicken for Growls. When we were both full and healthy, we proceeded toward the highest mountain.

At the mountain base was my dig site. I made a pit stop there to organize my items and raise the durability on my equipment. Once that was done, I began my ascent. I was jumping up block by block for what felt like forever. I covered dirt, stone and snow to reach the top. Passing through the clouds felt so surreal, but I couldn't get caught up in the moment. I was almost there. I bounced from one block to the next, placing dirt bridges when needed. When I leapt onto a small, flat surface, I knew I had reached the top. The enderman stood before me. With its back turned to me, it held a block of pure diamond over its head. It was as if it was showing it off to the world.

I didn't want to delay this any longer. I took out my sword and jabbed it into the enderman's back. It faced me, mouth open, but never moved from its perch like it was too stubborn to step down and face me. I took advantage of this and curved my blade across its chest. It fell with one, last gasp of breath. I reached forward and claimed its eye. Only one more left. My task was almost complete. A small smile crept onto my face, but it instantly faded. Approaching me from behind was a static screech. I flipped around to see the last enderman, mouth ajar, convulsing in fury. In its hands was a block of primed TNT. My eyes widened in horror as it sprinted toward me. In the last instant, I flung myself off the cliff.

I could hear and feel the massive explosion above me as I fell. But what rang out clearest of all was a small whimper from a dog. No. No, no, no. I landed in the dirt halfway down the mountain. Once I had my bearings I clambered frantically back up. When I reached the top, the smoke was beginning to clear. The mountaintop had become a crater filled with rock and soil. I scanned the entire desolate area for any sign of my dog. All I found was the last eye of ender floating in the rubble. I picked it up and stared into it. This little orb had cost me Growls. Images of all our adventures ran through my mind. And I couldn't help it, I cried. However, I didn't cry for some dog in a game. I cried for a lost friend. All the feelings of loneliness that Growls had suppressed now welled up inside of me. I crumpled to the ground in despair.

I wasn't sure how long I stayed on the mountaintop, but I didn't really care. The endermen had their revenge, and I felt no need to go on. The whole adventure meant nothing without someone to share it with. I sat in the crater gazing across the horizon. I had heard the sound of teleportation behind me. I didn't look. I knew who it was. Herobrine had come and stood beside me. I didn't acknowledge him. A few minutes passed by, and he placed a book by my feet. I picked it up with a sigh.

The portal awaits.
Will you see this through to the end?

His words infuriated me. Had he no sympathy? Couldn't he understand my loss? I know Growls was just a dog, but to me, he was special. He was my only friend in this whole wide world. He just couldn't be replaced. I took out a book of my own and began to write.

Why should I go to the end?
What's the point of any of this?
I don't understand you.
I just lost my best friend.
I'm completely alone now.
I just don't get what is so important about all this.
Why do I have to go through all of this?

I don't want to play this game anymore.
Go find another player to bother.

I threw the book at him in a huff. Herobrine looked from the book, to me, then back at the book. In a few moments he gave me a new book.

You are never alone in your hardships.
Your proof of this lies in The End.
Do you know the ender's purpose?
They guard something very special.
They play to your fears to keep you away.
But you are stronger than them.
I know because I was once like you.

I reread the words over and over. This was the most Herobrine had ever said to me. I wanted to believe him, but the sadness in me protested. I had to reason with myself. Why shouldn't I go to The End? I really did have nothing left to lose. A part of me truly wanted to see what the endermen were hiding. I knew I couldn't stay here forever, even though I wanted to. I took a deep breath, and gave Herobrine a small nod. He nodded in return and teleported away. I rose to my feet and hiked down the hill.

I traveled back to my house to prepare. The old homestead never felt so empty. I shook my feelings out of my head. I had to remain undistracted. In the kitchen, I crafted some golden apples. This place was going to be chock-full of endermen, so I had to be ready for anything. I thought about turning in for the night but rejected the idea. My stomach was in knots, and I was anxious to get this over with. I left the house and made way for the darkened woods. Zombies and spiders had blocked my path, but they were easily eliminated. I reached the shack and popped down the ladder. My footsteps echoed in the stronghold's corridors. I entered the room of the portal and placed the remaining eyes of ender in the slots.

The portal formed into an ominous black void. Unlike the nether portal, it was silent and unfeeling. I swallowed my fear and stepped in. When I had emerged, I was in a land of pure darkness. It was void of water and plant life. The endermen who wandered the place randomly appeared to be the only life-forms on this rock. I analyzed the terrain taking note of the obsidian towers speckled across the surface. The towers were varying in height, so I approached a shorter one. On its top was some sort of flaming crystal. I climbed up the tower to get a closer look. As I did, the mysterious crystal began to emit some sort of ray of energy. The ray seemed to be locked onto a target behind me. I spun around.

Soaring above me was a gigantic dragon of the purest black. Its sharp, purple eyes pierced through the darkness, and its booming roar shook the land. I felt that I was looking at fear incarnate. Herobrine didn't expect me to slay this beast, did he? The longer I watched the creature, the weaker I felt. I observed its movements wondering what I should do. I noticed that whenever it flew near an obsidian tower, the crystal would emit a ray on it. Were they healing it? I drew my sword and hit the crystal next to me. It exploded in a fiery blaze, knocking me off the tower. I quickly devoured a golden apple before I burnt to death. Note to self: crystals explode.

With one crystal destroyed, the dragon was alerted to my presence. It homed in on me, snarling deeply. I clambered out of its path just in time. It flew off and swerved around. Now that I had its attention, I knew there was no other option but to fight. The crystals seemed to be the key to weakening it. I drew my recently crafted bow and aimed at the top of the nearest obsidian tower. I shot three arrows, with the third one hitting the crystal. It blew up, and I was set upon again by the dragon. It dive-bombed me, knocking me into the air along with a few endermen. It was clear the dragon had no compassion for its supposed comrades.

I got to my feet and proceeded to the next crystal. This one went down in two arrows. My aim was improving. The dragon once again bashed me into the ground. This cycle continued until the last crystal was destroyed. With no way to regenerate its health, the dragon was in an uproar. Those violet eyes locked onto me with pure hatred. With it now vulnerable, my confidence returned. I could beat this thing. I drew my bow all the way back and shot it in the head. It screamed in pain and swooped down on me. I attempted to dodge, but its wings clipped me. I chomped on a golden apple as it made a U-turn. The dragon soared low to the ground, attacking me head-on. I swapped out my bow for my diamond sword. In one upward strike, I pierced the belly of the beast. It escaped toward the sky. This was where I wanted it. My bow came out, and one arrow flew straight into the dragon's throat.

The dragon froze in midair. A vibrant purple light erupted from its body. The monster gave its dying breath as the light tore the beast apart from within. The scene left me awestruck. It was done. My eyes closed as my relief came out in one long breath. When I opened them, the endermen surrounded me. One stood out from the crowd and neared closer to me. It spoke in a series of gurgling noises that at first didn't make any sense, but as I listened harder I could make out a few words.

You defeated our master.
You can have but a glimpse.
Anymore will kill you.
May you one day wake from the dream.

The enderman pointed behind me. I saw a bedrock structure that resembled a fountain. I peered inside to see the same black void of the End portal. My eyes shot back to the enderman. It nodded. I nodded in return and jumped into the void without looking back.

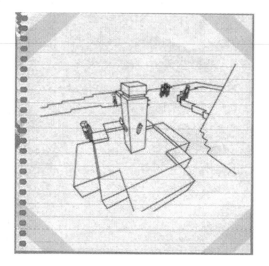

I felt like I was falling forever. It was dark. I couldn't even tell if my eyes were open or not. I fell in complete silence until, suddenly, words began to appear in front of me. When I read a line, a voice spoke. Another line was read, and a different voice spoke. Two people were having a conversation. It was about me. They knew my name. I was reading their thoughts like words on a screen. They spoke about the universe and other things I couldn't comprehend. They addressed me personally and told me a story. I hopped from one dream to another as the universe spoke to itself. I had played the game well, they said. I was not separate from everything else, they said. The universe loved me, they said. And then, I woke up.

I was inside my home, and I saw with a clarity never experienced before. I wandered outside and over the hills as if seeing them for the first time. I sat all by myself on a cliff overlooking the clearing, but I did not feel alone. I had bathed in the brine of the universe and became a hero. My senses had grown, and the world and I breathed in unison. I could hear the familiar teleportation behind me. I looked behind me, expecting to see Herobrine, but instead I saw a lone, floating book. I grasped it gently in my hands.

Do you understand things a little better now?
I'm sure you do. After all, you have beaten the
game.
This will be the last time we will cross paths.
Look upon yourself now, and see all that you are
and what you can become.
-Herobrine

I wordlessly closed the book. Look upon myself . . . I slowly switched myself to third-person view.

Made in the USA
Middletown, DE
07 December 2015